Adele
the Voice
Fairy

Special thanks to Narinder Dhami

No part of this publication may be reproduced, stored in a retrieval system, or transmitted in any form or by any means, electronic, mechanical, photocopying, recording, or otherwise, without written permission of the publisher. For information regarding permission, write to Rainbow Magic Limited c/o HIT Entertainment, 830 South Greenville Avenue, Allen, TX 75002-3320.

ISBN 978-0-545-48475-6

Previously published as *Pop Star Fairies #2: Adele the Singing Coach Fairy* by Orchard U.K. in 2012.

All rights reserved. Published by Scholastic Inc., 557 Broadway, New York, NY 10012, by arrangement with Rainbow Magic Limited.

12 11 10 9 8 7 6 5 4 3 2 1   13 14 15 16 17 18/0

Printed in the U.S.A.   40

This edition first printing, March 2013

Adele
the Voice
Fairy

by Daisy Meadows

SCHOLASTIC INC.

Jack Frost's Ice Castle

Campsite

Girls' tent

Main Stage

Karaoke tent

Café

The Harbor

Rainspell Island

It's about time for the world to see
The legend I was born to be.
The prince of pop, a dazzling star,
My fans will flock from near and far.

But superstar fame is hard to get
Unless I help myself, I bet.
I need a plan, a cunning trick
To make my stage act super-slick.

Seven magic clefs I'll steal —
They'll give me true superstar appeal.
I'll sing and dance, I'll dazzle and shine,
And superstar glory will be mine!

Contents

A Picnic Surprise

"What a fantastic place for a picnic!" Rachel Walker exclaimed, her face breaking into a huge smile.

She and her best friend, Kirsty Tate, were standing on a grassy hill above the site where the Rainspell Island Music Festival was taking place. The girls were camping there for five fun-filled days.

Below them, the two friends could see an enormous stage surrounded by lighting and sound equipment.

Close by was Star Village, where festival-goers were able to try being superstars themselves. The village had a karaoke tent as well as a small stage for dance classes. There were other areas where people could try out hairstyles and makeup, and even design their own stage costumes. There were souvenir stalls and food tents, too, and a campsite for festival-goers where Rachel, Kirsty, and Rachel's parents were staying.

"OK, girls," called a voice behind them. "The picnic's ready!"

Rachel and Kirsty spun around eagerly. Their friends Serena, Lexy, and Emilia, otherwise known as the famous singing group The Angels, were sitting on a fluffy pink picnic blanket, smiling up at them.

Rachel's and Kirsty's eyes grew wide as
they saw plates and bowls of delicious
food surrounding the three girls. Yum!

"Oh, this looks so glamorous!" Kirsty
sighed as she and Rachel joined The
Angels on the picnic blanket. There
were fancy triangular sandwiches and a
crystal bowl filled
with ripe red
strawberries
next to another
bowl of whipped
cream. A pitcher
of freshly made
lemonade with
floating ice cubes
and slices of lemon
stood in the cool
shade of a nearby tree.

"Well, you two *are* our special festival guests," Emilia reminded her, passing Kirsty a plate piled high with tiny sandwiches. Kirsty and Rachel had known The Angels ever since they'd won a competition to meet the band. Since then, they'd all become good friends.

Lexy was pouring lemonade into sparkling crystal glasses. "Rainspell Island is nice, isn't it?" she remarked. "So green and peaceful."

"It's a really magical place," Rachel agreed, glancing at Kirsty.

Rainspell Island was where the two girls had first met on vacation — and it was even more special, because it was also where they had discovered that fairies were real! Since then, the girls had shared many thrilling adventures with their tiny magical friends.

"We have another surprise for you, girls," Serena said when they'd finished eating. She took two books out of the picnic basket, one bound in pink silk and one in pale blue. The word AUTOGRAPHS was embroidered in swirly gold letters across the front of each book.

"We thought you might like to collect autographs from your favorite festival acts," Lexy explained as Serena handed the blue book to Kirsty and the pink one to Rachel.

"Thank you!" Rachel gasped, her eyes shining.

"You'll sign our books, won't you?" Kirsty asked eagerly. "Because you're our *very* favorite act!"

"We already have!" Serena replied, smiling. "Take a look."

Rachel and Kirsty quickly flipped open their books. The Angels had signed the first pages of each, and they'd also added the first few lines of their hit song, "Key to My Heart." Together, the two girls began to read the words aloud, and The Angels sang along:

"When I'm with you I feel so glad,
The truest friend I ever had,
I know we two will never part,
And that's the real key to my heart!"

But The Angels' voices sounded
hoarse and out of tune. Lexy, Emilia,
and Serena looked at one another in
dismay as they struggled to hit the
right notes.

"That was awful!"
Lexy exclaimed.

"Well, we *did*
perform at the
opening concert
this morning,"
Serena pointed
out. "Maybe we
strained our voices
a little."

"Yes, that must be it," Emilia agreed. Rachel and Kirsty didn't say anything, but they exchanged a secret, worried glance. They both knew *exactly* why The Angels' voices were so off-key. . . .

When Kirsty and Rachel had arrived at Rainspell Island earlier that day, they'd had a wonderful surprise. Their old friend Destiny the Rock Star Fairy had arrived to invite them to watch the rehearsals for the Fairyland Music Festival. Destiny had whisked the girls off to Fairyland to meet the seven Superstar Fairies. Their magic helped Destiny make sure that music everywhere was fun and in tune.

But at the rehearsal, the Superstar Fairies hadn't been able to perform well because sneaky Jack Frost and his goblins had stolen their seven magical music clefs. Jack Frost had declared that he was going to use the amazing powers of the magic clefs to become the biggest superstar in the world! Then he and his goblins had vanished in a flash of icy magic to Rainspell Island.

Rachel and Kirsty had agreed to help the fairies retrieve the magic clefs, knowing that music in the human and the fairy worlds would never be the same again if they didn't find them all.

"Maybe we should rest and let our voices recover," Lexy suggested.

"That's a good idea," replied Serena.

"We'll pack up the picnic supplies," Kirsty offered.

"Thanks, girls," said Emilia. "Listen, did you know that the band A-OK is performing later? The boys in the band are friends of ours, and I'm sure they'd love to sign your autograph books."

"Great!" Rachel exclaimed. "Kirsty and I love A-OK."

"Why don't you go to their rehearsal tent?" Serena suggested.
"You should be able to get in with those backstage passes we gave you."

"We'll see you at the A-OK concert later, girls," said Lexy, and The Angels set off down the hill, waving.

"The rest of the festival will be ruined if we don't find the missing clefs," Kirsty said with a frown as she and Rachel began collecting the empty plates.

"At least we found Jessie the Lyrics Fairy's clef this morning," Rachel said. "That means that superstars won't mess up their lyrics anymore."

"It was lucky that Jessie's clef had *just* enough magic to make The Angels' concert a success, wasn't it?" said Kirsty. "But we need to find all the clefs to make everything right again."

"Which means we have to keep an eye out for goblins at all times," Rachel replied.

After Jack Frost had stolen the seven clefs from the Superstar Fairies, he gave some of them to his goblins to hide.

Kirsty reached for the picnic basket to put everything away. But suddenly there was a whooshing sound as a burst of dazzling fairy sparkles shot out of the basket.

"Kirsty!" Rachel cried as she spotted a tiny figure dancing through the glittering mist. "It's Adele the Voice Fairy!"

Jax Tempo Has a Temper!

Adele greeted the girls with a wave of her hand. She wore a dark pink tunic over a floaty violet-colored blouse with ruffled sleeves, and she had sparkly pink ballerina flats on her feet. Her shiny hair was chestnut brown and pulled into a neat bun.

"Hello, girls," Adele called, zooming toward them. "I'm so glad you enjoyed your picnic, but I heard The Angels trying to sing along with you. All the stars at the festival will be singing off-key like that if I don't find my magical music clef — and fast!"

"We haven't seen Jack Frost yet, Adele," Kirsty told her. "But he must be here *somewhere*."

"Maybe he's hiding because he knows we're after him," Rachel said.

"I just know my magic clef is close by," Adele murmured wistfully. "Will you help me look for it, girls?"

Rachel and Kirsty nodded and smiled.

"We were about to go and watch A-OK rehearse," Kirsty explained. "We'll keep an eye out for goblins on our way."

"Perfect!" Adele said. "We can walk through the festival grounds and look for Jack Frost at the same time. But first, I should clean up for you before we go."

With one flick of Adele's wand, the plates, bowls, glasses, and picnic blanket rose up into the air and packed themselves neatly inside the basket.

"There are so many people around, I'd better hide," Adele decided. Rachel opened her backpack and the little fairy flew inside, perching on top of Rachel's autograph book.

"Let's go, girls!" Adele called.

Rachel and Kirsty each took one handle of the picnic basket and headed down the hill. Star Village was packed with people eager to try out the karaoke tent, the dance classes, and all the other activities. The girls hurried through the crowd toward the backstage area, where the rehearsal tents and the stars' trailers were set up. They dropped the picnic basket off at The Angels' silver trailer. Then they began to walk through the backstage area, searching for any sign of Jack Frost or his goblins. Suddenly, Kirsty heard someone singing a familiar rap song:

"I'm no fool
It's the number-one rule,
I'm supercool!"

"Oh, we heard that song this morning in the karaoke tent!" Kirsty exclaimed, stopping to listen. "It's that new rapper Jax Tempo."

"It sounds great!" Rachel said thoughtfully. "But where's it coming from?"

Kirsty pointed to an ice-blue trailer nearby. "Look, that trailer has JAX TEMPO written on the door," she replied.

Rachel and Kirsty
followed the sound
of the music over
to the trailer.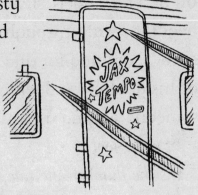

"Jax Tempo
must be inside,"
whispered Kirsty.

"Do you think he'd be
annoyed if we asked for his autograph?"
Rachel asked.

Kirsty shook her head. But before she
or Rachel could knock on the door, the
rapping inside the trailer stopped
abruptly.

"No, no, NO!" Jax Tempo yelled
angrily. Rachel and Kirsty recognized
his voice from earlier that day. "You're
all supposed to do the background
harmonies — you're not supposed to join

in with my rap! Gobby, do you hear me? Stop trying to take over my song!"

Rachel and Kirsty glanced at each other with disappointment.

"Jax Tempo's really angry," Kirsty whispered.

"We'd better not bother him if he's in such a bad mood!" Rachel murmured. "Let's go, Kirsty."

The girls turned to leave. But as they did, the door of the trailer suddenly swung open with a crash!

A-OK Is Not OK!

Rachel and Kirsty looked around curiously and saw a boy stomp out of Jax's trailer. The boy wore a bright green hoodie and a matching baseball hat pulled down low, hiding his face.

"I'm going to join a different band, and then Jax Tempo will be sorry!" the boy muttered grumpily. "All he does is complain about my singing. He just doesn't realize how talented I am!"

"That must be Gobby," Rachel whispered as she and Kirsty walked past him.

Kirsty nodded. "Look, Rachel, there's the A-OK rehearsal tent," she said, spotting it up ahead.

She and Kirsty stopped to find their backstage passes. As Rachel took hers out of her backpack, Adele smiled and waved.

"We're keeping our eyes open for your magic musical clef!" Rachel whispered to her.

The girls hurried over to A-OK's

rehearsal tent
and showed
their passes to
the security
guard outside.
As they went in,
Kirsty thought she
heard the sound of
scurrying footsteps close behind them.
She glanced around, but didn't see anyone.

"That's funny," Rachel said a few
seconds later, as they made their way
into the main part of the tent. "I thought
I felt something brush against me, but I
must have imagined it because there's no
one here except you and me."

"And A-OK, of course!" Kirsty
whispered. "Look, there they are,
standing near that piano!"

The four members of A-OK — Jeff, Amir, Rio, and Finn — were gathered behind the piano. Rachel and Kirsty stopped shyly on the other side of the room and gazed at the boys' familiar faces with delight. There was also an older man with black hair and dark, flashing eyes seated on the piano bench. As the girls watched, the man shook his head in despair.

"That was *terrible!*" he announced dramatically. "Again, please." He played an introduction and the four boys cleared their throats, then began to sing.

*"I'd climb the highest mountain,
Just to be with you,
I'd swim the deepest river,
Just to be with you. . . ."*

Rachel and Kirsty recognized the song as one of A-OK's biggest hits, but just like The Angels, the boys' voices sounded off-key. Looking furious, the man stopped playing.

"That was even worse!" he announced.
"You sound more like a bunch of farm
animals than a singing group. People
will blame *me* if they hear such a horrible
noise. Me, Alto Adams, the best voice
coach in the world! Now . . ." He stood
up from the piano and glared at the
boys. "Listen to this note
and sing it after me."
Alto Adams
took a breath
and then tried to
sing one note.
But, like the
boys, his own
voice was raspy
and completely
out of tune. Alto
looked horrified.

"What's happening?" He groaned. Sinking down into his seat again, he pounded on the piano keys in frustration. "The concert is starting soon. What are we going to do?"

The members of A-OK glanced at one another in despair, but said nothing. As the girls quietly took their autograph books out of their backpacks, Rachel could see that Adele looked miserable.

"No superstars here or in Fairyland will be able to sing beautifully ever again, unless I find my magic clef!" Adele whispered sadly.

Just then, Rio looked their way and saw Rachel and Kirsty waiting patiently nearby, autograph books in hand.

"Sorry you had to listen to that, girls," Rio said, shrugging his shoulders apologetically. "We're not usually this bad, are we, guys?"

The others shook their heads.

"Nothing's going right today, for some reason." Jeff sighed. "Even Alto's having problems." They all  glanced over at Alto, who was sitting on the piano bench and pouting.

"I hope we're not interrupting your rehearsal," Kirsty said.

"No way!" Finn replied. "We're glad to take a break."

"Do you think we could have your autographs?" asked Rachel.

"Are you sure you still want them after hearing us sing?" Amir joked, but Rachel and Kirsty could see that he looked just as anxious as the others.

Jeff, Amir, Rio, and Finn gathered around and signed the girls' autograph books. Then they handed the books back to Rachel and Kirsty, who thanked them, smiling widely. And then, right at that

moment, something magical happened. A clear, beautiful voice came out of nowhere, filling the tent with its melodious singing:

"I'd climb the highest mountain,
Just to be with you,
I'd swim the deepest river,
Just to be with you. . . ."

Alto Adams leaped up from the piano bench. "Who's that?" he demanded. "Come out and show yourself!"

Rachel and Kirsty could hardly believe their eyes when Gobby crawled out from under the piano.

"Gobby must have snuck past the security guard when we came in," Rachel murmured to Kirsty. "So we *weren't* imagining things!"

The members of
A-OK were staring
at Gobby in
amazement, too.
Excitedly, Alto
rushed over and
slapped him on
the back. "Wow,
your singing is
wonderful!" Alto
exclaimed. "In fact, it's A-OK!" And he
beamed at Gobby.

Confused, Rachel turned to Kirsty. "I
don't get it!" Rachel murmured. "How
can Gobby sing so well when Adele's clef
is missing?"

The A-OK boys had gone over to
congratulate Gobby on his great singing,

too. Gobby puffed out his chest, looking very happy with himself.

"So can I join the band?" he asked Alto eagerly.

"Of course," Alto agreed, shaking Gobby's hand. "We'd be honored to have you."

"Hooray!" Gobby yelled, jumping up and down with glee. As he did, Kirsty noticed a necklace fly out from the neck of his hoodie. Kirsty's heart

began to pound with excitement. She could see that the charm on the necklace was Adele's missing magic clef!

"Gobby's a goblin, and he has Adele's clef!" Kirsty whispered, pointing out the necklace to Rachel. "*That's* why he can sing so well."

"No wonder poor Jax Tempo was in such a bad mood," Rachel remembered. "Gobby was probably up to all sorts of mischief in his trailer! But how are we going to get the magical clef back from Gobby without anyone seeing?"

Gobby
the Star!

Frowning, Rachel and Kirsty looked at each other, wondering what to do.

"Stand next to the piano while I play, and sing the song straight through," Alto told Gobby.

"All right," Gobby agreed. "Can I have a brand-new outfit for the show?"

"With a voice like that, you can wear whatever you want!" Alto told him.

As Gobby began to sing, Rachel pulled Kirsty aside a little.

"What Gobby just said gave me an idea," Rachel whispered. "But we need to get out of here quickly, because we'll need Adele's magic to help us."

Quietly, the girls slipped out of the tent and then hurried around to the back of it, out of everyone's sight. There, Rachel opened her backpack and Adele fluttered out.

"I heard everything you said, girls,"

Adele cried. "Gobby the goblin has my clef, and that's why he has such an amazing singing voice!"

"I have an idea about how to get your clef back, Adele," Rachel told her. "Can you change me and Kirsty into fairies?"

"No sooner said than done!" Adele replied. With one wave of her wand, a puff of rainbow-colored fairy dust transformed the girls into fairies with glittery wings as beautiful as Adele's.

"We have to find A-OK's trailer," Rachel said as the girls zoomed up into the air.

"It's probably pretty close to the rehearsal tent," Kirsty suggested. The three of them flew higher into the sky so that they wouldn't be spotted by the people below, and then began circling the backstage area. Soon, they spotted a large gold trailer with A-OK written in black glitter on the door.

Adele pointed her wand at the door, and a stream of fairy sparkles unlocked it. The door opened just enough so that Adele and the girls could slip inside.

The trailer was very long, with a bathroom and a seating area at one end. At the other end, each A-OK member had his own dressing room. In each one there was a big mirror surrounded by lights, and a glittery sign with the band member's name on it. Their stage costumes were hanging on hooks.

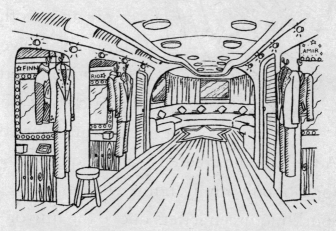

"Gobby will want his *own* dressing room," Rachel said with a grin. "Adele, could you make one for him?"

Adele nodded. There was a space between Amir's and Jeff's dressing rooms that had piles of spare clothes stacked in it. Adele briskly waved her wand, and the clothes lifted up into the air and neatly hung themselves on an empty clothes rack that was out of the way. More of Adele's magic created a dressing room for Gobby with his name written in sparkling green letters above the mirror.

"Gobby needs a stage costume," said Rachel. "I guess it will have to be green, or he won't like it! Any ideas, Kirsty?"

"How about some green sneakers with bolts of white on the sides?" suggested Kirsty.

Adele nodded and conjured up a pair of emerald-green sneakers with dazzling white lightning bolts.

"Maybe he'd like some dark green jeans," said Rachel. "Oh, and a belt with a G-shaped gold buckle?"

Adele flicked her wand and the jeans and belt joined the sneakers in Gobby's dressing room. The girls then added a green and purple hoodie and a matching baseball hat.

"And now for the most important thing of all," said Rachel. "Adele, we need a clef necklace, exactly like yours."

"But without the magical powers, obviously!" Adele said, her eyes twinkling. A mist of fairy glitter swirled briefly around in the air. Then the necklace appeared, hanging on one of the hooks. Rachel smiled. "We have everything we need except Gobby!" she declared. "Let's go and find him."

The three friends flew out of the trailer, and Adele locked the door again with her magic. They headed for the A–OK rehearsal tent, but on the way there they heard shouts and cheers coming from over by the stages.

"What's that noise?" asked Rachel, hovering in midair.

"Look at that little stage over there," Kirsty said. "There's a crowd of fans around the A-OK boys — and Gobby's with them!"

Staying high up in the air so that no one could see them, Adele, Rachel, and Kirsty flew over to the stage. It was surrounded by life-size cutouts of the four boys, posters of the band, and booths selling A-OK T-shirts, CDs, and programs. Rio, Finn, Jeff, and Amir were signing autographs and chatting with the fans who were crowding around the stage — and so was Gobby! Rachel, Adele, and Kirsty could see that the goblin was enjoying every moment, posing for photos and scribbling his name in autograph books.

"Gobby, it's great that you joined A-OK!" called a girl from the crowd. "But are you feeling nervous about the concert later? You look a little green!"

"Um — I'm so excited about being in A-OK, I feel sick!" Gobby replied. "But I'm sure I'll be all right when I get onstage later."

"Can the band sing something for us right now?" another fan shouted eagerly. There were cheers of delight at this suggestion.

"You'll have to wait for the concert, folks," Alto told the crowd of fans. "The boys need to rest their voices now."

The fans looked disappointed, but they continued clamoring for autographs, shouting questions at the band, and snapping pictures with their cell phones. They all wanted photos of the band's newest member, Gobby.

"Gobby's loving all the attention!" Adele whispered to Kirsty and Rachel. "How on earth are we going to get him away from all his new fans?"

"I have an idea!" replied Kirsty. "Listen, this is what we'll do. . . ."

Kirsty's Clever Plan

Adele, Rachel, and Kirsty flew to hide behind one of the T-shirt booths. There, out of sight, Adele's magic returned the girls to their human size. Then Adele hid herself in Rachel's backpack, and the two girls hurried out to join the crowd of fans around A-OK.

"Hi, Gobby!" Kirsty called, smiling up

at him. "We saw you earlier today, remember?"

"We didn't realize you were such a big star!" Rachel added. She waved her autograph book in the air. "Can we please have your autograph?"

"Of course!" Gobby agreed graciously, holding out his hand. "And will you please sing something for us?" Kirsty added, giving him her autograph book. Gobby shot an anxious glance at

Alto Adams on the other side of the stage.

"I'm not supposed to sing anything until the concert," he muttered as he scrawled his name in the book.

"Oh, *please*?" Rachel pleaded.

"You have such a wonderful voice!" Kirsty added.

Looking very pleased with himself, Gobby cleared his throat and sang softly:

"I'd climb the highest mountain,

Just to be with you,

I'd swim the deepest river,

Just to be with you. . . ."

But Gobby didn't look quite as pleased when Rachel and Kirsty instantly clapped their hands over their ears. The girls had horrified expressions on their faces.

"Is there something wrong with your

51

voice, Gobby?" Rachel asked with a frown.

Gobby stared at her in disbelief. "No!" he snapped. "Why?"

"Because you sound awful!" Kirsty told him. It wasn't true at all. Gobby's voice was still beautiful, but Kirsty had a plan.

"No, I don't!" Gobby gasped. He fumbled at the neck of his hoodie, feeling

 for the magic clef as if to make sure it was still there. "My singing is *amazing*!" Rachel and Kirsty shrugged and glanced at each other. "Maybe you're just feeling a little nervous about the concert later," Kirsty suggested.

"Yes, you need to relax a little," Rachel added. "I bet you have a fabulous costume all ready for you in the A-OK trailer. That'll make you feel like a real star!"

Gobby cheered up instantly and nodded. "Yes, maybe I should go and check it out," he said thoughtfully.

"We'll come with you," said Kirsty, winking at Rachel. "We know where the trailer is. We saw it earlier today."

Gobby slipped off the stage and hurried away without Alto Adams or the other boys noticing. The girls went with him, leading the way to the trailer. Then Rachel and Kirsty saw a very faint cloud of shimmering fairy dust. Adele peeked out of Rachel's backpack and used her magic to unlock the door again!

"Oh!" Gobby gasped with delight as he climbed into the trailer and saw the dressing rooms. "Look, it says GOBBY over there on that glittery sign!"

"There are your new clothes for the concert, hanging on those hooks," Kirsty said, pointing.

Gobby smiled from ear to ear and rushed over to look at his outfit more closely. He seemed thrilled with the jeans and hoodie and the gold belt with the G buckle. But then Gobby noticed the copy of the clef necklace hanging on one of the hooks. Rachel and Kirsty saw him frown and begin to sing softly:

"I'd climb the highest mountain,
Just to be with you,
I'd swim the deepest river,
Just to be with you. . . ."

Gobby seemed to be making sure that
the magic of the clef necklace he was
wearing was still working. Rachel and
Kirsty immediately groaned loudly
and shook their heads in despair.

"What's the matter?" Gobby
demanded angrily.

"Your voice sounds awful, Gobby!"
Rachel exclaimed. "I hate to tell you
this, but your singing is really bad!"

Just Like Magic!

Gobby looked very angry. Meanwhile, Kirsty picked up the fake necklace and slipped it over her head.

"That necklace makes you look like a superstar, Kirsty!" Rachel exclaimed admiringly. "Why don't you try singing a song?"

"OK!" Kirsty said with a grin. She
began to sing:

"When I'm with you I feel so glad,
The truest friend I ever had,
I know we two will never part,
And that's the real key to my heart!"

Kirsty knew she sounded terrible, but
Rachel cheered and clapped loudly.

"I never realized you had such a great

singing voice,

Kirsty!" Rachel

declared.

Gobby was looking

very confused.

"I think the other

goblins have been

playing a trick on me,"
he murmured to himself.

Then he pointed at Kirsty. "I want *that* necklace!" Gobby announced. "This one I'm wearing doesn't work anymore!"

"Are you sure, Gobby?" Kirsty asked innocently.

"Yes, I'm sure!" Gobby snapped. He pulled off Adele's necklace and threw it to the floor. Instantly, Adele zoomed out of Rachel's backpack. Swooping down, she caught the necklace before it hit the ground. It immediately shrank to its fairy size.

Gobby gave a shout of rage. "It's a fairy trick!" he yelled, stomping his foot. He barged out of the trailer, almost knocking over the A-OK boys as they came  through the door. Jeff, Amir, Finn, and Rio looked very surprised! Adele quickly flew to hide inside Rachel's backpack again, clutching her magic musical clef and beaming happily.

"What's the matter with Gobby?" asked Amir.

"He brought us here to see his costume," Kirsty replied. "But it looks like he's changed his mind and he doesn't want to be in the band after all!"

"That's too bad," said Finn. "But we were practicing our songs on the way over here, and just as we reached the trailer, our singing voices came back!"

"It was like magic!" Jeff added. Rachel and Kirsty laughed. The A-OK boys had no idea just how right they were!

The concert took place later that afternoon. Rachel and Kirsty were lucky enough to get places right at the front of the stage, and they danced and sang along to all of A-OK's songs with the rest of the crowd. Adele joined in, too, still hidden inside Rachel's backpack. Because she was nearby, there was just enough magic around to ensure that the concert was a success!

As A-OK finished with one of their well-known hit songs, accompanied by a spectacular dance routine, Rachel and Kirsty clapped and cheered until their hands were sore and their throats were hoarse.

The A-OK boys took a bow and then bounded off the stage. Rachel and Kirsty moved away from the crowd, and then Adele popped up out of Rachel's backpack.

"Wasn't it a great concert, Adele?" asked Rachel with a grin. "Thanks to your magic!"

Adele smiled, too, touching the clef that hung around

her neck. "It was wonderful," she replied. "But we need to find *all* the magical clefs to bring harmony back to superstars everywhere!"

"We'll keep looking, Adele," Kirsty assured her.

"Thank you!" Adele called. Then, with a flick of her wand and a friendly wave, she was whisked off to Fairyland.

"Five more magical clefs to go!" Rachel remarked, as she and Kirsty made their way back to the Walkers' tent. "Do you think we'll find another one today, Kirsty?"

"I hope so!" Kirsty replied.

THE SUPERSTAR FAIRIES

Adele has her magic clef back.
Now Kirsty and Rachel need to help

Vanessa
the Choreography Fairy!

Join their next adventure
in this special sneak peek. . . .

Festival Fun

"Hooray!" cheered Rachel Walker, as she and her best friend, Kirsty Tate, walked along Rainspell Beach. "The sun is shining, we're on vacation together, *and* we're at the Rainspell Island Music Festival."

"It's been wonderful so far, hasn't it?" Kirsty agreed with a smile.

It was certainly turning out to be a day the girls would never forget. First, they'd seen their favorite band, The Angels, open the show. Next to perform was the boy band A-OK, who had wowed the crowd with their melodic harmonies. And best of all, Kirsty and Rachel had found themselves caught up in an exciting new fairy adventure, this time with the Superstar Fairies!

"Hi, girls," chorused three familiar voices.

Rachel and Kirsty turned to see Lexy, Serena, and Emilia — also known as The Angels.

"Hi," said Kirsty. She and Rachel had met the band a while ago, when they'd helped Destiny the Rock Star Fairy. Now they were friends. The girls in the band had even given them backstage passes to the festival! Being friends with pop stars was almost as much fun as being friends with the fairies!

"Did you see A-OK? Weren't they fabulous?" said Lexy.

"I didn't know they were such great performers," said Emilia, kicking off her sandals and wiggling her bare toes in the golden sand. "Those boys rocked!"

"I can't wait to see Sasha Sharp tonight," Rachel added. "She's such a good dancer."

"Sasha's amazing," Serena agreed. "Have you seen the video for her new song, 'Let's Dance'? She does such a cool routine. How does it go again?"

The Angels started singing Sasha's latest hit, and they all tried to remember the dance moves. . . .

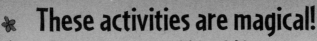

These activities are magical!
Play dress-up, send friendship notes, and much more!

SCHOLASTIC
www.scholastic.com
www.rainbowmagiconline.com

HiT entertainm

RMAC

RAINBOW magic™

There's Magic in Every Series!

The Rainbow Fairies
The Weather Fairies
The Jewel Fairies
The Pet Fairies
The Fun Day Fairies
The Petal Fairies
The Dance Fairies
The Music Fairies
The Sports Fairies
The Party Fairies
The Ocean Fairies
The Night Fairies
The Magical Animal Fairies
The Princess Fairies
The Superstar Fairies

Read them all!

■ SCHOLASTIC

scholastic.com
rainbowmagiconline.com

RMFAIRY7

SPECIAL EDITION

Three Books in Each One— More Rainbow Magic Fun!

Joy the Summer Vacation Fairy
Holly the Christmas Fairy
Kylie the Carnival Fairy
Stella the Star Fairy
Shannon the Ocean Fairy
Trixie the Halloween Fairy
Gabriella the Snow Kingdom Fairy
Juliet the Valentine Fairy
Mia the Bridesmaid Fairy
Flora the Dress-Up Fairy
Paige the Christmas Play Fairy
Emma the Easter Fairy
Cara the Camp Fairy
Destiny the Rock Star Fairy
Belle the Birthday Fairy
Olympia the Games Fairy
Selena the Sleepover Fairy
Cheryl the Christmas Tree Fairy
Florence the Friendship Fairy
Lindsay the Luck Fairy

■ SCHOLASTIC
scholastic.com
rainbowmagiconline.com

HIT entertainment

RMSPECIAL